THE BOY WHO CRIED WOLF

TONY ROSS

Andersen Press

THIS BOOK BELONGS TO:

. . . .

For Zoë and Katy

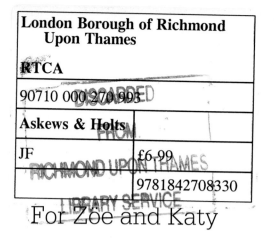

This paperback edition first published in 2008 by
Andersen Press Ltd.
First published in Great Britain in 1985 by Andersen Press Ltd.,
20 Vauxhall Bridge Road, London SW1V 2SA.
Published in Australia by Random House Australia Pty.,
Level 3, 100 Pacific Highway, North Sydney, NSW 2060.
Copyright © Tony Ross, 1985
The rights of Tony Ross to be identified as the author and illustrator
of this work have been asserted by him in accordance with the
Copyright, Designs and Patents Act, 1988.
All rights reserved.
Colour separated in Switzerland by Photolitho AG, Zürich.
Printed and bound in Singapore by Tien Wah Press.

10   9   8   7   6   5   4   3

British Library Cataloguing in Publication Data available.

ISBN 978 1 84270 833 0

Once upon a time a little boy lived on this side of the mountains. His name was Harry.

On the other side of the mountains a wolf lived in the lap of luxury. Nobody ever asked *his* name.

The wolf had fine manners (for a wolf).
Sometimes he put on his dinner jacket . . .

and came over the mountains . . . for dinner.

Because the wolf liked dining on people, everybody on this side of the mountains was afraid of him. So . . .

whenever Harry had to do something he hated,
like having a bath,

he would cry, **"Wolf!"** (even if the wolf was nowhere to be seen).
Because everybody was afraid of the wolf ...

Harry was left alone to do just what he wanted.

Once a week Harry went for his violin lesson.
Because he hated lessons . . .

he cried, **"Wolf!"** even though the wolf was not around.

Then Harry was left alone to play the kind of music *he* liked.

Sometimes Harry even cried, **"Wolf!"** just for the fun of it.

One day Harry was cycling in the mountains when
the wolf jumped out of the rocks.

"Wolf!" cried Harry.
He ran back to the town crying, "WOLF! WOLF!"
all the way.

"WOLF!" cried Harry, but his grandmother didn't believe him. Harry always cried, **"Wolf!"**
"Tell me another one!" she said.

"WOLF!" cried Harry, but nobody listened.

"Save me from the **WOLF!**" shrieked Harry,
but everybody laughed.
"Harry's crying 'wolf' again," they said.

At last the wolf caught up with Harry.
"You shouldn't have told so many lies!" said the
grown-ups sternly.

The wolf heard the grown-ups and changed his mind about eating Harry.

He ate the grown-ups instead.

Then . . .

he changed his mind again and had Harry for supper.

C'est la vie.

Also illustrated by Tony Ross:

9781849397629

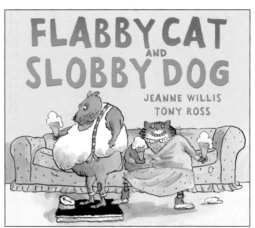

9781842709825

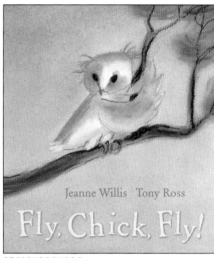

9781849394383

9781842709450

9781849394161

9781842707111